BOOK 2c
The Ladybird Key W

I like to write

by W MURRAY
with illustrations by MARTIN AITCHISON

Ladybird Books

Jane can write.

The answers are on Page 46

Peter c__ write.

I c__ write.

Toy shop

ball dog

et

Jane

and

6

They can write.

T___ like to write.

T___ write for fun.

The answers are on Page 46

Peter writes for fun.

Jane writes f__ f__.

I like to write f__ f__.

The answers are on Page 46

Peter and Jane
Doll Toy shop

ball

9

Jane says,
Here you are, Peter

Peter and Jane
Toy shop

dog   ball

The answers are on Page 47

Peter says,
Here y__ a__, Jane.
Here y__ a__, they say.

11

Jane writes.

I want to fish.

Pat wants to come.

We w___ to go
to the water, P____.

The answers
are on Page 47

12

Here they go.

They go to the water.

They g_ to f___.

15

Here comes Pat.

Here comes P__,
the dog.

P_ _ c_ _ _ _ to Peter
and Jane.

Here they come.

Here comes Peter.

The answers are on Page 48

Here comes Jane.

Here comes Pat.

Look here, Peter says.

Look here, he s___.

The answers are on Page 48

The fish can jump.

L___, the f___ can j___.

The ball is in the water.

Go for it, says Peter to Pat.

The answers are on Page 48

G_ for i_, h_ says.

Pat jumps
into the water.

23

Pat jumps
into the water.

He jumps i___ the
water f__ the ball.

He likes it
in the water.

This is fun, says Peter.

T___ is fun, he says.

The answers are on Page 49

We like fun.

W_ like f__
in the water.

Yes   No

1 Is Jane here ? __.

The answers are on Page 49

2 Is Peter here ? ___.

3 Is the dog here ? __.

4 Has Peter a fish ? __.

Yes   No

1 Are Peter and Pat here ? __ .

2 Is Jane here ? ___ .

3 Is this a toy shop ? ___ .

4 Has Jane a tree ? __ .

The answers are on Page 49

Yes   No

1 Has the dog some water ? _ _ _.

2 Can the dog write? _ _.

3 Can toys jump? _ _.

4 Have Peter and Jane some fish ? _ _ _.

The answers are on Page 49

Yes   No

1 Are Peter and Jane
  in the tree ? _ _ .

2 Can Peter jump ? _ _ _ .

3 Are the fish in the
  water ? _ _ _ .

4 Is the ball in the
  water ? _ _ .

The answers are on Page 50

① ② ③ ④

Finish the sentences with the help of the pictures.

1 The dog wants ___ ____.

2 Jane looks for ___ ____.

3 Peter is in ___ ____.

4 Peter and Jane look in ___ ____.

the fish	the ball
the tree	the shop

The answers are on Page 50

Finish the sentences with the help of the pictures.

1 Peter and Jane like _____ .

2 Here are some ____ .

3 Peter writes to ____ .

4 Jane likes ___ ___ .

| sweets | toys |
| Jane | the dog |

The answers are on Page 50

① ② ③ ④

Dear Jane,
Yo

39

Here are Peter and Jane.

They want to go home.

You and I want to go h___, says Peter.

Yes, we want to go h___, says Jane.

Pat, the dog, w____ to go home.

The answers are on Page 51

Write out correctly—

1 Peter I Look, can says, jump.

2 water Jane some wants.

3 some They sweets have.

4 home Peter Jane and are.

Flash cards may be helpful with these exercises

The answers are on Page 51

43

Write out correctly—

1 write wants to Jane.

2 fish for Peter look likes to.

3 dog fun This likes.

4 the in is water Pat.

Flash cards may be helpful with these exercises

The answers are on Page 51

45

Pages 46 to 51 give answers to the written exercises in this book. They can also be used for revision and testing, before proceeding to Book 3a.

Pages 4/5

Jane can write.

Peter can write.

I can write.

Page 7

They can write.

They like to write.

They write for fun.

Page 8

Peter writes for fun.

Jane writes for fun.

I like to write for fun.

Pages 10/11

Jane says, Here you are, Peter.

Peter says, Here you are, Jane.

Here you are, they say.

Page 12

Jane writes.

I want to fish.

Pat wants to come.

We want to go to the water, Peter.

Page 14

Here they go.

They go to the water.

They go to fish.

Pages 16/17

Here comes Pat.

Here comes Pat, the dog.

Pat comes to Peter and Jane.

Pages 18/19
Here they come.
Here comes Peter.
Here comes Jane.
Here comes Pat.

Pages 20/21
Look here, Peter says.
Look here, he says.
The fish can jump.
Look, the fish can jump.

Pages 22/23
The ball is in the water.
Go for it, says Peter to Pat.
Go for it, he says.
Pat jumps into the water.

Page 24
Pat jumps into the water.
He jumps into the water for the ball.
He likes it in the water.

Pages 26/27

This is fun, says Peter.
This is fun, he says.
We like fun.
We like fun in the water.

Pages 28/29

1 Is Jane here? No.
2 Is Peter here? Yes.
3 Is the dog here? No.
4 Has Peter a fish? No.

Page 30

1 Are Peter and Pat here? No.
2 Is Jane here? Yes.
3 Is this a toy shop? Yes.
4 Has Jane a tree? No.

Page 32

1 Has the dog some water? Yes.
2 Can the dog write? No.
3 Can toys jump? No.
4 Have Peter and Jane some
   fish? Yes.

Page 34

1 Are Peter and Jane in the tree? No.

2 Can Peter jump? Yes.

3 Are the fish in the water? Yes.

4 Is the ball in the water? No.

Page 36

1 The dog wants the fish.

2 Jane looks for the ball.

3 Peter is in the tree.

4 Peter and Jane look in the shop.

Page 38

1 Peter and Jane like sweets.

2 Here are some toys.

3 Peter writes to Jane.

4 Jane likes the dog.

Page 40

Here are Peter and Jane.

They want to go home.

You and I want to go home, says Peter.

Yes, we want to go home, says Jane.

Pat, the dog, wants to go home.

Page 42

1　Peter says, Look, I can jump.

2　Jane wants some water.

3　They have some sweets.

4　Peter and Jane are home.

Page 44

1　Jane wants to write.

2　Peter likes to look for fish.

3　This dog likes fun.

4　Pat is in the water.

New words used in this book

Total number of new words 27

Pages 46, 47, 48, 49, 50 and 51 contain answers, and can be used for revision and as test pages.